The FRENCH FRY KING

Rogé

Tundra Books

Published in Canada by Tundra Books
75 Sherbourne Street, Toronto, Ontario M5A 2P9

Published in the United States by Tundra Books of Northern New York
P.O. Box 1030, Plattsburgh, New York 12901

Library of Congress Control Number: 2011934163

Library and Archives Canada Cataloguing in Publication

Rogé, 1972-
[Roi de la patate. English]
    The french fry king / Rogé.

Translation of: Le roi de la patate.
ISBN 978-1-77049-350-6

    I. Title. II. Title : Roi de la patate. English.

PS8635.O394R6313 2012   jC843'.6   C2011-905206-7

We acknowledge the financial support of the Government of Canada through
the Book Publishing Industry Development Program (BPIDP) and that of the Government of Ontario through the Ontario Media Development Corporation's Ontario
Book Initiative.

We further acknowledge the support of the Canada Council for the Arts and the
Ontario Arts Council for our publishing program.

ONTARIO ARTS COUNCIL
CONSEIL DES ARTS DE L'ONTARIO

Printed and bound in China

1 2 3 4 5 6   17 16 15 14 13 12

The FRENCH FRY KING

For Caro

Roger was a long sausage dog with big ideas. He liked to wander around town asking himself all sorts of unusual questions.

Questions like:

"If I had a human girlfriend, would we hold hands or paws?"

"If humans were dogs, would they build doghouse skyscrapers?"

"If there are sausage dogs, are there sausage humans?"

Roger was NOT the kind of dog who chased mail carriers, or chewed bicycle tires, or barked at cars. That was boring.

Instead, Roger preferred to think!

If I were a human, he thought, *I could be an astronaut, a tap dancer, a country and western singer or — why not — maybe even a barber!*

But, since he was just a dog, Roger sighed,
"Ah! Life is so unfair!"

One beautiful evening, while Roger was thinking on a park bench, something very important happened. An old lady left a trail of potatoes as she passed by.

As they rolled along the ground, Roger cried out, *"Woof!* I have an idea!"

Without another thought, Roger took matters into his own paws!

He found an old caravan and worked night and day fixing it up. Then he began peeling hundreds of potatoes — thinking all the while: *When I am finished, I will be rich! Rich enough to visit every city in the world!*

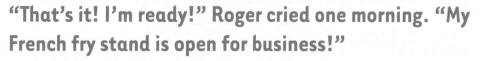

"That's it! I'm ready!" Roger cried one morning. "My French fry stand is open for business!"

The delicious smell drew crowds of French fry fans.

"I've never eaten fries as good as these!" said the police officer.

"This dog's cooking skills are exceptional," said the crossing guard.

And the priest who was passing by said, "Heavenly! Just heavenly!"

Word spread. Roger's French fry stand captured the hearts of the whole town.

"SAUSAGE DOG FLIES WITH THE SUCCESS OF HIS FRIES," the newspaper declared.

One radio announcer named the town: Home of the World's Best Fries!

On television, a woman claimed: "One serving of Roger's French fries cured my arthritis!"

With all this enthusiasm, Roger began thinking even bigger thoughts. He decided to share his cooking skills with the world.

From PEI to Idaho, and all the way through Mexico, people enjoyed Roger's French fries.
In India, Roger served curried fries.

In Kenya, they came dipped in chocolate.
In Vietnam, they came with soy sauce.
In Cuba, they were served with salsa.
And at the New York Stock Exchange, the value of French
fries rose higher and higher....

Roger's fries were known around the globe. Everyone
declared Roger the French Fry King!

When he returned home from his travels, the entire
city was there to welcome him: "Hurray! Bravo! Long
live the king!"

Roger was triumphant. His paws didn't touch the
ground for days. He was, without doubt, the most
successful sausage dog on the planet!

But one rainy day, out of the blue, Roger realized he had grown dissatisfied all over again.

It had been wonderful to see the world and to have been crowned king, but his boredom had, sadly, returned.

Deep in thought, the sausage dog sighed again. "Ah! Life is very strange."

There was nothing to do but to abandon his French fry stand. He walked the streets as he had in the past. "People only love me for my fries," he said to himself. Lost in his own glum thoughts, Roger walked right into a street sign.

"Oowww!"

With his vision still a little blurry, he managed to read: "Charlotte the Corn Cob Queen."

The French Fry King approached the queen, and asked for a cob of corn. It took only one bite to know, "I have never eaten such delicious corn in all my life!"

"Why don't you try my helium-popped popcorn?" Charlotte asked. "Last week, the baker floated up into the air after eating it."

Roger was amazed!

Every day after that, Roger visited Charlotte. He told her fantastic stories about his travels abroad. He told her about the spaghetti fries he served in Italy, and about the super-frozen fries that were so popular in the North Pole.... He told her everything. Charlotte was enthralled, and Roger forgot to be bored.

Little by little, Roger found himself falling in love. For the first time in his life, no questions or bothersome thoughts pestered him. He finally confessed to Charlotte that he loved her.

All the newspapers on the planet carried the news.

Before long, the French Fry King and the Corn Cob Queen opened a brand-new stand!
   Roger and Charlotte's Royal Shepherd's Pie!

"Woof! Life is beautiful!"